# Porter Flies
# UP, UP, AND AWAY

Porter

## Debi Moon

Illustrated by: JP Roberts

Debi Moon

◆ FriesenPress

Suite 300 - 990 Fort St
Victoria, BC, V8V 3K2
Canada

www.friesenpress.com

ISBN
978-1-5255-4072-1 (Hardcover)
978-1-5255-4073-8 (Paperback)
978-1-5255-4074-5 (eBook)

*1. JUVENILE FICTION, TRANSPORTATION, AVIATION*

Distributed to the trade by The Ingram Book Company

**Hi my name is Porter.** Grandma tells me I am a lucky boy because I am going to get to fly in an airplane. I fly my little plane as high as I can reach, but Grandma says the plane that will take me to Boston to see my Aunt Linny and Uncle Alex will be real, not a toy. The real plane will lift me high into the sky, up into the clouds and closer to the Moon.

I like the Moon. I want it to be closer. "Grandma, how will a plane get me up to the Moon?"

"A plane is a remarkable flying machine," explains Grandma. "You can sometimes hear a plane when it flies over your house but it is so high up it appears to be small, like a toy. When it lands on the ground though, it is very large. It is bigger than a whale, bigger than your Daddy's monster truck and bigger than the house you live in. The plane can carry many more people than you, your baby sister, and your Mom and Dad. It has to carry lots of people who are travelling on holiday or visiting family and friends, just like you."

I asked Grandma, "Can I touch the Moon?"

"I am sorry Porter, you will be on the inside of the plane so you will only be able to touch the Moon and clouds with your eyes. Only astronauts have actually touched the Moon."

I asked Grandma, "Will Daddy and an astronaut be driving the plane?"

"Your Dad will drive you to the airport in your car, but it will be a pilot and co-pilot that will be steering the plane. They will be wearing a special cap and uniform."

4

"I want to be a pilot. I can steer the plane! "Grandma, can Luna be my co-pilot."

"Woof, woof," barked Luna in agreement, as she raced away to fetch her flying cape.

Grandma laughed at Luna's enthusiasm, telling me Luna doesn't have wings with which to fly.

"One day Porter, when you finish school, you can get your pilot's license and take Luna flying."

I asked, "Why do we need wings, Grandma?"

"Everything that flies have wings and so, of course flies have wings as well as buzzing bees and tweeting birds. Your Daddy's monster truck has a large motor but doesn't have wings, so it can't fly. A whale is large indeed, is a powerful swimmer and can jump very high out of the water but its fins are not wings and so it cannot fly."

"But Grandma," I said, "I don't have wings, so I can't fly!"

"Remember Porter, the plane has wings. If you had wings and could fly, you would be dive-bombing people and splatting poo on their shoulders. You would have so much fun that I would never get you back down to earth. I prefer you just as you are, without wings, so I can have you close by. We can play and share hugs whenever we want to."

I tell Grandma that Mommy and Daddy got me a new backpack to carry on the plane. "Grandma, it's a robot! I will show you."

Daddy says I'm a big boy now and I can help carry luggage. I am to pack my toothbrush and extra underwear and shorts. Mom says I can even put snacks in my bag. I love Mom, she's the best Mom ever.

I ask Grandma, "Can I put Luna in my backpack too?"

Grandma says that Luna would wriggle around in the backpack and likely eat all my snacks. She said, "Luna will still be here with Grandpa and I when you come back home to us."

I wish Grandma and Grandpa and Luna could come on the plane with me.

I told Grandma, "I don't like saying goodbye."

Grandma tells me she will miss me too and I am to send lots of pictures showing how much fun I am having with Aunt Linny and Uncle Alex in Boston. Grandma says she will have Luna howl at the Moon and when I look up into Boston's night sky, I might be able to hear her.

Grandma said, "Porter, instead of saying goodbye, we could do our special 'wiggle jiggle'."

I like that. We start with elbow kisses and eye winks, followed by thumbs up or down and we end with a wiggle jiggle of our bums. Thumbs up is when Grandma and Grandpa come to visit and stay over-night so I can wake them up in the morning. If we do thumbs down, it means Grandma and Grandpa must go home and I won't see them when I wake up. The bum wiggle always makes us laugh. Grandma says, "No one, including us can be sad when they see our bum wiggle jiggle."

I asked Grandma, "When can I see my big plane?"

Grandma explained that after Daddy drives us to the airport, where many planes land and take off, we will meet with a special security officer. He will be wearing a uniform too.

"This officer will ask some very important security questions. He might ask you your name, where you live, and who you might be visiting in Boston. You will have to show the officer what is inside your backpack, so it's a good thing Luna won't be there."

"Then can I see my plane?" I asked.

"Yes Porter. The officer will stamp your new passport book, the one with your picture. You can give him a high five if you want and then you will be allowed to see your plane."

**Grandma was right!** I see a long hallway and big windows. I must get closer. I race towards the glass windows and my eyes are filled with planes, really big planes with large wings.

"Mommy, I can see all my planes! Mommy, Daddy come quick and see. I found my plane. Daddy, it really is bigger than your monster truck."

Grandma said I am going to like flying and I will see what a bird sees when it flies high over my head. Grandpa teased me, telling me I may need to flap my arms and pretend I have wings, to help the plane lift. They said I will feel the power of the plane as its engines roar like an angry Tyrannosaurus chasing us down the runway as the plane climbs up, up and away.

"Just like when Daddy lifts you up high over his head and pretends to drop you; flying in a plane is just as giggle worthy" said Grandma. "It can be scary and fun at the same time."

## My Plane just flew up into the clouds and I give Mommy and Daddy a great big toothy smile, my cheesy smile as Grandma calls it.

I have my own seat on the plane, right beside Mommy and Daddy and my new baby sister. I smile at her, showing her not to be afraid. Grandma says we will be kept safe by being together and wearing our seatbelts, just like when I am in the car. I have my own table to put my snacks and colouring books on. I have my very own computer screen so I can watch cartoons and I hear them with my smiley-face head- phones that

Aunt Linny got for me. I look out the small window, searching for the Moon. There are many stars in the night sky and there it is, the Moon. It is a big ball of white and I smile at Mommy.

## "See the Moon, Mommy?"

"I sure do, little man, says Mommy. "I sure do."

"Mommy can you find me a bathroom? Grandma said the plane doesn't have a tree for me to pee on, like when I am camping at the 'bush'."

"I sure can, little man," says Mommy. "I sure can."

When I get back to my seat, a nice lady asks if I would like a drink and a cookie. "Yes, please." I look at Mommy and remember to say thank you. Mommy smiles at me.

Grandma said my eyes will grow tired and that its helpful to have a nap, to prepare me for all the walking in airports. Just as I close my eyes, I see Luna flying by outside my window, with her cape straight out behind her and pterodactyl on her back, flapping its wings. Luna is smiling her toothy grin at me. I must remember to tell Grandma that Luna got her wings.

Mommy wakes me up and hands me my backpack. She has a twinkle in her eye as she tells me we have landed. We walk off the plane into a new airport. I am tired and my legs don't want to walk. We go through a door and suddenly there they are.

"It's Aunt Linny and my Alex! My Alex, it's you, you're really here!"

I race to him and he lifts me up high and gives me hugs.

Aunt Linny says, "Porter, it's you, you're really here! Welcome to Boston."

After more hugs they help Mommy and Daddy carry baby sister and all our luggage. They lift me up to ride on the cart on top of the luggage. My eyes want to close again, but I can't let them.

"Porter?"

"Yes, Grandma?"

"When you wake up," she whispers, "can our next flying adventure be in a hot air balloon?"

"No, Grandma, a helicopter! Can Luna come too?"

At the beach

Ice cream inside the
Red Sox helmet.

Steering a boat
in the harbour

Riding the whale at The
Greenway Carousel

Two thumbs up for the
Boston Red Sox ball game

Boston Fire Truck

CPSIA information can be obtained
at www.ICGtesting.com
Printed in the USA
LVHW070759250220
648065LV00002B/3